D0819843

The Christmas Pups

Teresa Bateman

Illustrated by John Kanzler

Albert Whitman & Company, Chicago, Illinois

Library of Congress Cataloging-in-Publication Data

Bateman, Teresa.
The Christmas pups / by Teresa Bateman ; illustrated by John Kanzler.
p. cm.
Summary: Left by the side of the road just before Christmas, three puppies are brought
to a shelter where an older dog tells them how to get adopted,
but the two boys decide to misbehave to assure that their sister will find a home.
ISBN 978-0-8075-1160-2
[1. Dog adoption—Fiction. 2. Animal shelters—Fiction. 3. Dogs—Fiction.
4. Animals—Infancy—Fiction. 5. Christmas—Fiction.] I. Kanzler, John, 1963- ill. II. Title.
PZ7.B294435Chr 2011 [E]—dc22 2010046089

The design is by Carol Gildar.

For more information about Albert Whitman & Company,
please visit our web site at www.albertwhitman.com.

For Evan, Evan, William, and Reagan—welcome to the warm arms of a loving family!—T.B.

For Lorelei.—J.K.

Icy rain fell. Cars roared by as three puppies shivered in a cardboard box that was slowly falling apart.

Ruff and Tuff crouched against their little sister, Penny, trying to block the wind. They had been in a car, too, before their box was dumped. Where were they now?

"I'm hungry," Tuff said. A horn blared.

"It's not safe here . . ." Ruff barked, but where could they go? What could they do? All they could see was pavement, lights, and the rain turning to snow.

Headlights caught the box. Ruff poked his nose over the top. Brakes squealed.

A warm scarf wrapped around them. They were gently placed in the back seat of a car. Confused, but too tired to worry, they curled up as the *ka-chunk ka-chunk* of the wheels lulled them to sleep.

Ruff, Tuff, and Penny blinked awake in a warm pen.
Next door an older dog smiled. "Welcome to the shelter.
I'm Brownie. Now have something to eat and drink, and
Merry Christmas."

"Where are we?" Ruff yipped.
"Is there more food?" Tuff yapped.
"What's Christmas?" Penny asked.

The older dog settled down. "Christmas is ginger cookies under the table, red glittery tree balls you're not supposed to play with, and a stocking with your name on it. It's twinkly lights, sweet songs, gifts for those you love, and being with family."

"It sounds wonderful," Penny sighed.

"It is," Brownie agreed. "And it's coming tomorrow. Lots of people give puppies as gifts. Behave, and you'll find out about Christmas."

"What about you?" Penny asked.

"People like puppies best," Brownie replied. "Don't worry about me. I've had my share of Christmases. Things have a way of working out. This year it's your turn."

Ruff, Tuff, and Penny yipped in happy anticipation. They tumbled and played for a bit, then plopped into a pile. As Penny fell asleep, Ruff nudged Tuff.

"Let's give Penny a family for Christmas," he whispered.

Tuff blinked. "She has a family—us."

"But we don't have a home. She might get one. We're the only puppies here," Ruff pointed out. "Brownie says people pick puppies. If you and I are bad, people will have to pick Penny."

"But we won't be together," Tuff whispered.

"We won't anyway," Ruff replied sadly. "Nobody's going to take three puppies. Let's just do our best to make sure Penny gets a family for Christmas."

The noise woke them a little later. "It's time!" Brownie announced.
Dogs were barking. Cats in the next room were meowing.
"Time for what?" Penny asked.

"Time for people to choose pets," Brownie said softly. "This is the last day before Christmas. Now remember what I said. Behave!"

Ruff, Tuff, and Penny watched as other animals were taken into the arms of smiling families, but it seemed nobody wanted them.

"Puppies are too much work," they heard more than once.

It was a long day. A few people seemed interested in the puppies, but Ruff and Tuff didn't think they were a good fit.

They wanted the perfect family for Penny for Christmas. So whenever hands reached in for them, Ruff and Tuff yipped and fought each other.

The day was almost over. "It looks like we're going to miss Christmas this year," Brownie sighed.

Ruff and Tuff licked Penny. Their plan had failed. "At least we're still together," said Ruff.

Just then the door opened again.

A family entered, two older boys elbowing each other and laughing. Behind them came a little girl, quiet but smiling.

"I want that one and that one and that one!" the boys cried, pointing everywhere.

Their mother shook her head. "This is your sister's present. She gets to choose. You two already have plenty of animals on the farm."

"It's not the same," one boy protested. "A horse can't sleep on your bed."

"And cows don't fetch sticks," the other added.

The puppies watched as the family moved closer. Ruff and Tuff looked at the little girl. She was quiet, like Penny. She was happy, like Penny. They nodded at each other.

When the family reached them, Ruff and Tuff nudged Penny forward.

"A puppy!" the little girl said.

"Three puppies," explained the shelter worker. "They came in together. Any of them would be a good choice."

Ruff and Tuff waited to get everyone's attention. Then they did their worst. They barked, bounced, and pounced on each other, making Penny look like the best-behaved puppy in the world.

"Those are GREAT puppies," said the two boys. "Look at them run, listen to them bark!"

Penny stared at her brothers. What were they doing?

Then she was scooped out and held in the little girl's arms. It felt just right. She licked the girl on the cheek. The girl giggled. Penny snuggled.

"Looks like a match to me." The worker smiled.

Ruff and Tuff kept barking and bouncing, just to be sure. "That's quite enough," Brownie ordered. "I see what you're doing. Now behave!"

They immediately settled down. Their plan was a success. Penny would have a family for Christmas!

She looked back at them as they yipped "good luck."
Ruff and Tuff tried to smile, knowing it would probably be
the last time they saw her.

"Why THAT one?" one of the boys asked as the door
closed behind them.

Ruff and Tuff slumped to the floor.

"We did it," Ruff said.

Tuff nodded, but whimpered a little. "At least we've got each other."

When the door opened again, Ruff and Tuff didn't look up.
It couldn't be for them.
But then two sets of excited yet gentle hands picked them up.

"This one's mine! This one's mine!" two voices shouted. "Thanks, Mom. Thanks, Dad!"

Ruff and Tuff looked up into the faces of the two boys.

The boys' mother shook her head. "What are we going to do with three puppies?"

Her husband smiled. "Maybe we need an older dog to keep them in line," he suggested, nodding to the pen next door. "There's plenty of room on the farm."

Brownie stepped out and rubbed against the man's leg.

Tuff looked at Ruff. "I guess things do work out, after all,"
he said with a happy yip. "Merry Christmas!"
"The merriest!" Ruff barked in return.